BERNARD WABER
Lyle at Christmas

Houghton Mifflin Company Boston

Walter Lorraine WL Books

Walter Lorraine (wL) Books

Copyright © 1998 by Bernard Waber

www.houghtonmifflinbooks.com

Library of Congress Cataloging-in-Publication Data
Waber, Bernard.
 Lyle at Christmas / written and illustrated by Bernard Waber.
  p.   cm.
 Summary: At Christmastime, Lyle the crocodile helps Mr. Grumps
search for his missing cat, Loretta.
   RNF ISBN 0-395-91304-7   PA ISBN 0-618-38002-7
   [1. Crocodiles—Fiction. 2. Cats—Fiction. 3. Lost and found
possessions—Fiction. 4. Christmas—Fiction.] I. Title.
PZ7.W113Lwc 1998
[E]—dc21
                                                    98-5381
                                                       CIP
                                                        AC

Printed in the United States of America
WOZ 10 9 8 7 6 5 4

Lyle at Christmas

Christmas was in the air.

It was everywhere.
And everywhere he went,
Lyle the Crocodile was wished
a merry Christmas.
Children gave him big hugs.

So did Millie, the crossing guard.
"That's my special Christmas hug,"
she told him.

Taxi drivers waved cheerily to him,

as did the newsstand owner,
and the pizza man.

Everyone loved Lyle the Crocodile.
And in return Lyle loved the whole wide world.
He loved Bird . . .

and Loretta the cat,
who lived
two houses away
with Mr. Grumps.

He loved East 88th Street, and the house he shared
so happily with Mr. and Mrs. Primm, their children,
Joshua and Miranda, his mother, and Bird.

His only problem
was deciding what gift
he wanted most.

But if Lyle was happy at Christmas, there
was someone living close by who was not at all happy.
That someone was feeling downright miserable, in fact.
And that someone was Mr. Grumps.

"I am having the blahs," moaned Mr. Grumps.
"Those low-down, pit-bottom, yech-ie, yech-ie holiday blahs.
'Tis the season to be jolly. Right? Well, tell me about it."

"Oh, I've tried so hard to get into the spirit of it all,"
Mr. Grumps groaned. "I trimmed the tree.
Wrapped gifts. Hummed a carol or two. Wished for snow.
Roasted chestnuts on an open fire. Did all of that.
And still, I am having the blahs."

Even his adored cat, Loretta, who mostly enjoyed
a sunny disposition, had had it up to her whiskers with
down-in-the-dumps Mr. Grumps and took to moping about.
In her darkest moments, she considered running away.

Everyone tried desperately to cheer Mr. Grumps.
Lyle exhausted his entire repertoire of sure-fire
amusing tricks. Nothing.

Joshua and Miranda baked a huge batch of happy-face
cookies for him, accompanied with a note that read:
Have a nice day. But Mr. Grumps was in no mood
for happy faces. Nor was he about to have a nice day.

Mrs. Primm thought
a game or two of checkers
would divert him, but she soon
discovered that Mr. Grumps
was a mighty sore loser.

Lyle's mother, Nurse Felicity,
checked Mr. Grumps' pulse
and asked him to stick out his tongue.
"No problem with his health,"
she concluded.

Mr. Primm tried telling him
uproarious jokes.
"Heard it," Mr. Grumps said,
cutting him short.
"Heard that one too."

It soon became painfully clear, at least for the moment,
that no amount of cheering could lift Mr. Grumps
out of his sorry, sorry holiday blahs.
"We'll just do all that we can to let Mr. Grumps
know, no matter what, that we do care about him —
and love him," said Mrs. Primm.

One day, a terribly distraught Mr. Grumps
appeared at the Primms' door.
"Loretta! Loretta! Oh, my poor, sweet, Loretta!" he cried.
"What's happened to Loretta!" Mrs. Primm exclaimed.
"She's gone; vanished; slipped out as I signed for a package.
Loretta is lost!" Mr. Grumps wept.

"Oh, no!" everyone cried out.
Loretta lost! Lyle was thunderstruck.
"Loretta! Loretta!" Mr. Grumps sobbed away.

Immediately, the family spread out
in search of Loretta.
Mrs. Primm circled the neighborhood
in her car.

Joshua and Miranda
questioned people
on the street.

Mr. Primm and Lyle
looked everywhere,
late into the night.
No Loretta.

No one slept that night.
Lyle kept a constant vigil at the window,
anxiously searching the street below
for signs of Loretta. Chilling visions of Loretta
wandering alone or caught up in all manner
of dangerous scrapes haunted him.

Suddenly Lyle knew all too clearly what he
wanted most for Christmas — but much sooner, please.
"I want the safe return of Loretta," he whispered to himself.

The next day, the family was
posting notices everywhere about Loretta
and handing out flyers.

Mr. Grumps offered a handsome reward,
and many strays were brought to his door.
"No, that's not Loretta. Sorry, not that one either.
Nor that one," he said, sadly turning one after
another away. "But do, please, try to find good homes
for these cats," he always urged them.

At long last, Mr. Grumps
had something meaningful
to be unhappy about.
"Where, oh where, is she?"
he cried out again and again.

So where indeed was Loretta?
Well, after spending a shivery, terrifying night
far away from East 88th Street,
she was, at this exact moment, having
serious second thoughts about running away.

True, she had had her fill of grumpy Mr. Grumps,
but now she began to miss him — miss him desperately,
blahs and all. And she missed her friends; but mostly Lyle.

The world away from home was a lonely place,
she sadly decided — especially at Christmas.

"Ah, what have we here?"
Loretta soon found herself
staring up at the grinning face
of Prunella Kitt,
known in the neighborhood
as the Cat Lady.

"And oh, so pretty," Prunella chortled.
"All alone, are you? No home?
No one to look after you — to feed you?
Oh, you poor, shriveled darling. Well, not to worry.
Prunella is here. And Prunella will take good care of you."

Prunella scooped Loretta up, put her in a basket,
and scurried home.

With quick steps Prunella climbed the rickety stairs
to her third floor rooms.

At the landing she met an upstairs neighbor.
And that neighbor was none other than
Hector P. Valenti, Star of Stage and Screen.
"Lookie-look will you," said Prunella, proudly lifting
the lid of her basket.
"Not another cat, Prunella!" Hector rolled his eyes.
"Yes, and isn't she a precious little lambkin!"
Prunella cooed in a baby voice.

"Adorable," Hector shook his head in disbelief
as he rushed off to work.

Prunella entered her apartment and
immediately set Loretta free.
"Welcome home, my darling," she said.
Loretta blinked with amazement.
It was instantly clear that Prunella never met a cat
she didn't like. Her place swarmed with cats —
cats here, cats there;
cats, cats, cats, galore, everywhere.

And some weren't at all nice.
Now, more than ever, Loretta longed
to be home.

Meanwhile, the search for Loretta went on.
Posting still another notice, Lyle and Mrs. Primm
suddenly heard a familiar voice call to them from inside
a house. They soon discovered the voice belonged to
Lyle's former dance partner, Hector P. Valenti,
Star of Stage and Screen.

The old friends were delighted to see each other.
But what was Hector up to now?
Well, at the moment it seemed he was very busy
cleaning windows.
"Oh, do you live here?" asked Mrs. Primm.

Hector came to the door.
"Actually, I work here," he answered.
"I perform star-quality housecleaning services.
It's an interesting little side venture — ahem,
between stage and screen engagements, of course."
"Yes, of course," said Mrs. Primm.

Lyle immediately gave Hector a flyer about Loretta.
Hector read it with great interest — especially the part
about the reward. He looked carefully at Loretta's picture.
Suddenly bells went off in his head.
"I can find Loretta," he announced.

Lyle and Mrs. Primm were overjoyed.
"Oh, please, let's get her at once," said Mrs. Primm.
"Not so fast" said Hector, "the people I work for
will want a clean house when they return."
"Oh, but we must find Loretta!" Mrs. Primm pleaded.

Hector had an idea. "Come in, please," he said.
Hector took off his apron and put it on Lyle.
"I'm sure you'll know what to do, Lyle," said Hector.

"I don't think Lyle should be doing this,"
said Mrs. Primm. But Lyle's cheerful smile
encouraged Mrs. Primm to leave with Hector.

"Good-bye, dear," said Mrs. Primm, "we won't
be long, I'm sure."
"See you later," said Hector. "And do, please,
remember to dust under the beds."

Lyle was so delighted at the prospect of finding Loretta,
he got to work at once — and with great enthusiasm.
He scrubbed the dishes thoroughly in hot sudsy water . . .

and admired
his reflection
in their gleaming
brightness.

After polishing the silverware, Lyle went on
to make the beds. As always, he was proud of
his hospital corners and pictured how pleased
the homeowners would be when they returned.

After that there was the usual scrubbing,
dusting, sweeping, and waxing.

To lighten his housecleaning chores,
Lyle decided to have fun with floor waxing
by pretending to do a television commercial.

"See my shiny waxed floor," he made believe he was saying.
"Isn't it beautiful? Isn't it gorgeous? Want to know my secret?
Dazzle. That's right folks, Dazzle Floor Wax. So if you want your
floor to sparkle like mine, rush out this very instant, if not sooner,
and get yourself some Dazzle. And do get the giant economy size.
Take it from Lyle, you won't be sorry. Oh, and by the way, friends,
remember our slogan: Dazzle Dazzles."

Lyle was so pleased
with his commercial,
he began to dance.

OOPS! The waxed floor was slippery, and he fell —
kerplunk! — at the feet of Mr. and Mrs. Worthmore,
the owners of the house, who had just come home.
They were not amused.

In fact, they were so astonished to find
a crocodile prancing about the house, Mrs. Worthmore
promptly fainted as Mr. Worthmore managed,
somehow, to call the police.

The police arrived and arrested Lyle.
He was charged with breaking in.
News of his arrest was broadcast
far and wide.

Later, in court, the judge was about to have
Lyle locked up when Mrs. Primm, Hector,
and Prunella burst in — with Loretta.
Lyle's eyes lit up the instant he saw Loretta.

"Please, your honor," Mrs. Primm pleaded,
"Lyle is innocent. He was merely helping to clean
so Hector could be free to find Loretta."
"Is this true?" asked the judge.
"Yes, your honor," said Hector.
"And where exactly was Loretta?" asked the judge.
"Safe and sound in my home," Prunella spoke up proudly.

When they heard this, Mr. and Mrs. Worthmore,
who were also in court, immediately dropped the charges.
They even commended Lyle for doing an outstanding job
cleaning their house.
"Best we ever had," said Mrs. Worthmore,
looking scornfully at Hector.
"Case dismissed," said the judge.

On Christmas Eve, Mr. Grumps gave a dinner party.
Everyone was invited: The Primms, Lyle and his mother,
Hector, Prunella, and even Mr. and Mrs. Worthmore.
Besides sharing the reward for finding Loretta,
Hector and Prunella seemed, also, to share a blossoming
fondness for one another.
"We will need to find good homes for your cats, Prunella,"
said Hector. "We'll be on the road so much, you know."
"Oh, of course, Hector, dear," Prunella answered, adoringly.

Mr. Grumps and Loretta were blissfully reunited.
"Friends, this is a most joyous, meaningful night,"
said Mr. Grumps, "and so, I say to one and all,
merry, merry Christmas —
and good-bye forever to the blahs."
Everyone smiled . . .

especially Lyle and Loretta.